Mighty

by Joan Holub
pictures by James Dean

SCHOLASTIC PRESS · NEW YORK

Dads

Library of Congress Cataloging-in-Publication Data Available

ISBN 978-0-545-60968-5

10 9 8 7 6 5 4 3 2 1   14 15 16 17 18

Printed in Malaysia   108

First printing, May 2014

Book design by David Saylor and Charles Kreloff

For Jeffrey Salane, a mighty amazing editor.

— J. H.

To my dad, Curtis Thomas, a self-taught artist who explained to me about internal combustion engines and wanted me to be a concert pianist. The one who inspired me to dream.

— J. D.

Mighty Dads,
strong and tall,
help their children,
young and small.

They keep them safe
and bolted tight
and show them how
to build things right.

**Excavator Big
helps little Vator dig.
They go**
scoop,
scoop,
scoop.

**Bulldozer Strong
shows Dozy right from wrong.
They go
roar,
roar,
roar!**

**Crane Long Arm
keeps junior Crane from harm.
They go**

reach,
reach,
reach.

Boom Truck Tall
helps Boomer crash a wall.
They go
crash,
bang,
boom!

Cement Mixer Busy
gives a hug if Mixie's dizzy.
They go

spin,

spin,

pour.

**Dump Truck Sturdy
teaches Dumpy to get dirty.
They go**
fill,
drive,
dump.

Backhoe Steady
waits for Hoe-Hoe to get ready.
They go
trench,
trench,
trench.

Grader True-Blue
makes room for Grady, too.
They go
smooth,
smooth,
smooth.

Steamroller Brave
shows little Roller how to pave.
They go
roll,
roll,
roll.

**Forklift Wise
cheers whenever Forky tries.
They go**
lift,
lift,
lift.

Now the young ones
join the crew.
And when their rumble
day is through —

Mighty Dads say,
"I'm proud of you!
Tomorrow let's build
something new!"